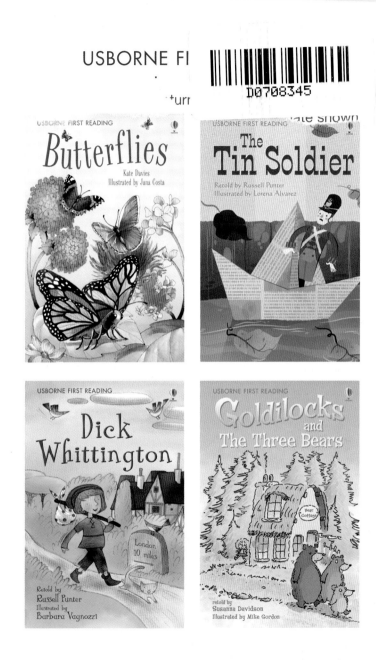

The Goose Girl

Based on a story by the Brothers Grimm

Retold by Russell Punter

Illustrated by Qin Leng

Reading consultant: Alison Kelly
University of Roehampton

Once there was a queen, with
a daughter named Rose.

Princess Rose was helpful...

and kind...

and she *never* broke a promise.

3

Rose had agreed to marry
Prince Hal. He lived in a
palace far, far away.

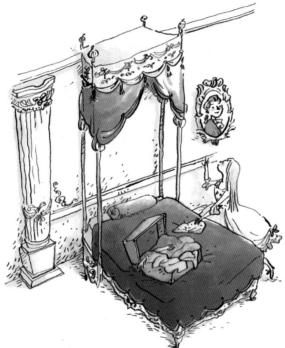

They had never even met.
Today, she was going to visit
him for the first time.

Before Rose left, her mother gave her a magical gift.

It's beautiful!

It was a singing locket.

I can see all that you do.
I will be a friend to you.

"Promise you won't lose
it," said the queen. "It will
protect you."

"I promise," said Rose.

Princess Rose set off with
her maid, Grizelda.

Grizelda moaned and
groaned all the way.

"Giddy up, you silly nag,"
she yelled at her horse, Dobbin.

Rose was much kinder to
her horse, Falada.

He wasn't like
other horses...

Falada could talk!

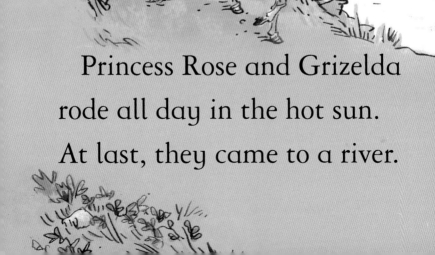

Princess Rose and Grizelda
rode all day in the hot sun.
At last, they came to a river.

"I'm so thirsty, Grizelda," said Rose. "Please would you get me some water?"

"Get your own!" snapped
Grizelda, rudely.

But Grizelda hadn't packed
Rose's cup. "I'll have to do
without it," thought Rose.

So she lay down on the
hard ground to drink.

If your poor mother only knew,
It would break her heart in two.

13

When Princess Rose
stood up...

...her locket fell in the
river and floated away.

"I'm going to tell the queen you lost the locket," said Grizelda, laughing.

"Please don't do that," said Rose. "I promised I'd look after it."

"Okay," said Grizelda.
"But only if you change
clothes with me."

So Rose swapped her pretty gown for Grizelda's scruffy old dress.

"Promise not to tell a living thing we changed places," ordered Grizelda.

I promise.

Soon after, they arrived
at the prince's palace. Hal
rushed up to Grizelda.

"Princess Rose?" he said.
"Yes!" lied Grizelda.

In the Great Hall, Hal's
father, the king, smiled at Rose.
"And who are you?" he asked.

"She's my maid," lied
Grizelda once again.

I'm fed up
with her.

Rose wanted to tell the
king the truth...

but she couldn't break her
promise to Grizelda.

Grizelda looked out of the window at Falada.

"That chatterbox might tell the prince who I really am," she thought.

"My old horse is worn out,"
she said. "Get rid of him, Hal."

"And find my lazy maid
some work," Grizelda added,
grandly.

"She could help Conrad,"
said the king.

"He looks after the
royal geese."

Yes! She can be
a goose girl.

27

The next morning, Rose and
Conrad took the geese to
the meadow.

On the way, Rose saw
Falada tied up in a field.

"Poor Falada," she cried.
"Poor Princess," said Falada.

Conrad had never seen a
talking horse before.

That was
weird.

"Why did it call you
'Princess'?" he asked.

"I can't say," said Rose.

At the meadow, Rose untied
her hair and began to brush it.

Conrad had never seen such golden hair.

He tried to snatch a handful. Rose quickly chanted a rhyme.

"Blow now, gentle wind I say. Blow this goose boy's hat away."

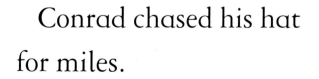

Conrad chased his hat for miles.

When he returned, Rose
had tied her hair back.

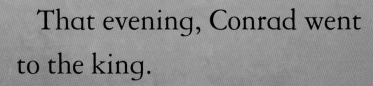

That evening, Conrad went
to the king.

"Do I have to work with that odd girl?" he asked.

Odd?

Conrad told him about the horse and his hat.

The next day, the king
followed Conrad and Rose.
He heard the talking horse...

Poor
Princess.

...and he saw Conrad's
flying hat.

That evening, the king
looked for Rose. "Are you
really a princess?" he asked.

"I promised not to tell a
living thing," sighed Rose.

"You could tell this cupboard," said the king.

I'll wait outside.

Rose climbed into the cupboard and told it her story.

The king heard everything.

When Rose came out,
the king took her to the
palace maids.

They gave Rose
a bubble
bath...

they did
her hair...

...and they found
her a beautiful
dress to wear.

That night, there was
a royal feast.

The king sat Rose next to
Prince Hal. Then Grizelda
marched in.

She didn't recognize Rose.
"Who's that?" she snapped.

"First, I have a question for
you," said the king.

"How would you punish someone who was cruel, rude and told lies?"

"Ha! I'd make them live in a stinky pigsty," said Grizelda, with a grin.

"Then that's what we'll do with you," said the king.

So Grizelda got what
she deserved.

And Rose married Prince Hal
– as promised.

The Goose Girl was first written down by two brothers, Jacob and Wilhelm Grimm, about two hundred years ago. The Grimm brothers lived in Germany and collected lots of folk tales.

Series editor: Lesley Sims

First published in 2012 by Usborne Publishing Ltd., Usborne House, 83-85 Saffron Hill, London EC1N 8RT, England. www.usborne.com
Copyright © 2012 Usborne Publishing Ltd.

48

USBORNE FIRST READING
Level Four

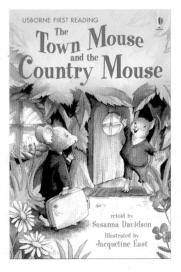

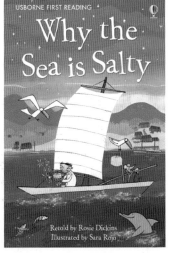